I0901521

# Writing Letters to Leaders

TAKING CIVIC ACTION

Leona Fowler

CIVICS FOR THE REAL WORLD™

Rosen Classroom™

Do you know what democracy is? Democracy is a kind of government. In a democracy, people have a say in how their country is run.

The people don't run the country directly. They have leaders called representatives. Representatives act for the people in government.

Representatives can work for the whole country. They can also work for states, cities, and even small towns.

Representatives listen to the people. They try to give the people what they want. Do you know who represents you?

Find out who your leaders are. If there's something you want changed, you can write them a letter!

The president is the leader of our country. If you want better laws, you can write a letter to the president.

Your city might need better roads. You can write a letter to the city mayor. If enough people ask, the mayor may get the roads fixed.

Is your park full of trash? Write a letter to your local leaders. Make sure to say why the park is important to your community.

You can even write letters to your school leaders. If you want better lunch foods, write a letter to your principal.

Writing letters to leaders helps create change. Think about what could be better in your community. Then, get writing!

# WORDS TO KNOW

letter

road

trash